John F. Layson

The Haunted Library

A Novocastrian Reminiscence

John F. Layson

The Haunted Library
A Novocastrian Reminiscence

ISBN/EAN: 9783744729383

Printed in Europe, USA, Canada, Australia, Japan

Cover: Foto ©Andreas Hilbeck / pixelio.de

More available books at **www.hansebooks.com**

PLATE I.

THE HAUNTED LIBRARY:

A NOVOCASTRIAN REMINISCENCE.

BY J. F. LAYSON.

WITH ILLUSTRATIONS BY THOS: MACKAY.

NEWCASTLE-ON-TYNE,
THE TYNE PUBLISHING COMPANY, LIMITED, FELLING.
1880.

MAWSON, SWAN, & MORGAN,
24, 30, & 32 GREY STREET.

" The Past but lives in Words ; a thousand ages
  Were blank, if Books had not evoked their GHOSTS,
  And kept the pale, unbodied Shades to warn us."
                                        —LYTTON.

THIS

→✳ REMINISCENCE ✳←

IS

HUMBLY INSCRIBED

TO

THE CHAIRMAN

AND

MEMBERS OF THE COMMITTEE,

AND TO

THE CHIEF LIBRARIAN

OF

𝕿𝔥𝔢 𝔓𝔲𝔟𝔩𝔦𝔠 𝔏𝔦𝔟𝔯𝔞𝔯𝔦𝔢𝔰

OF

NEWCASTLE-UPON-TYNE,

1880.

THE ARTIST'S ADDRESS.

An Artist, as all Readers ought to know,
Is not expected with his pen a show
To make of eloquence ; but rather he
Should ever with his pencil strive to be
The true exponent of his Author's work,
Lest ambiguity may therein lurk.
With such an object, I submit my lot
Of Drawings, taken on the very spot.

THE AUTHOR'S PREFACE.

ALTHOUGH 'tis now our purpose to relate
A Tale of Ghosts returned to mortal state,
We will not try the agony to pile
In hackneyed, harrowing, or hateful style :
But rather, lest a Reader should disdain
To scan our lines, will rigidly refrain
From either distant or overt allusion
To sepulture and charnel-house profusion.

LINES ILLUSTRATED.

THE ARGUMENT.

The Night-Side of Newcastle: Striking Effect by St. Nicholas. Provisional Protracted Payment. Study in Dun-Brown by our Scenic Artist: The Caterer, a Caution. A Still Night! Spirits about. Policemen not about, but still. Our Leading Actor appears, for this occasion only! Speech-making made easy. Firing of the Tower Battery. How to open a Public Library. Something like a Ghost-Scene: a Statue-tory Act in the Drama. Our Leading Actor gets into trouble through a Spirited Policy. A Precipitate Prison Act: all rights reserved. The Republic of Letters: Communistic overflow of Spirits. Celebrated Authors in the Press. A Supplement to *Noctes Ambrosianæ*, Dedicated to the BAT CLUB. The Union-Jacques is unfurled: James the First floats in air. A second James on the Staff! *N.B.*, Our Flagstaff is merely a Stump, but no Matter. Oratory: No Tax on Proof-Spirits. The Art of Book-Keeping taught in one lesson. Marriage: a Metaphor. Goldsmith is grandiloquent. Our Leading Actor is caught napping. Our Leading Actor is charged. An Explosion! How to Rise in the World. Friends in Adversity: Virtue is its Own Reward. True and Tried! The Sentence. Our Leading Actor is discharged. Medical Advice, gratis. Good Morning!

The Haunted Library:

A Novocastrian Reminiscence.

" Compelled, the tall, thin, half-starved Sprite
Shall earth re-visit, and survey
The Place where once his treasure lay."

—Churchill.

PLATE II.

I.

SAINT NICHOLAS had struck the midnight hour,
   High in the belfry of his massive tower,
      And old Newcastle, famed for Norman keep—
To keep no man from getting off to sleep—
Had sent her most intelligent Police,
Sir Robert Peel's own guardians of the peace,
Upon their beats, with stately helmets capped,
In order that night-prowlers might be trapped.

II.

For valid reasons, we shall not allude
To matters atmospheric, nor intrude
The threadbare weather question.   Still, a host
Of spirits, disembodied, Pandon's Ghost
Included, might have revelled on that night,
In playful glee ; and, with unfeigned delight,
Have urged beholders into Charon's Styx,
For laughing at their bold, fantastic tricks.

III.

A Baked-potato-man did homeward trudge,
With engine, donkey, cart, and inward grudge,
Because a gay Lothario, 'pon town,
Had ventured to affirm that half-a-crown
He tendered had, in payment for a meal
Of mealy tubers and stewed peas. Appeal
Had entered been—Proof heard—with oaths improper ;
Verdict : Defendant had cleaned out his Copper.

IV.

The last latch-key had turned, and last door handle,
Put out had been the last tom-cat and candle ;
The streets had been deserted by mankind—
The sharpest Serjeant could no Peeler find—
Pedestrians all had made their way to bed,
By Bacchus carried, or by Somnus led,
And Novocastria's embryonic City
Was silent—mute were Passion, Play, and Pity !

V.

But who is this that now the stillness breaks,
And ever and anon his cranium shakes ?
Who is 't that does, with muffled tones, rehearse
To-morrow's speech in—anything but verse ?
A Senator ! In cogitation deep,
He hums and mutters as if half-asleep.
Up Pilgrim Street he slowly treads his way,
And sighs for glory and the coming day.

Though patients claimed his daily, hourly care,
He finds his patience melting into air.
Ha, ha! He, he! Hi, hi! Ho, ho! Hu, hu!—
He *(sotto voce)* cries—If I'd my due,
To-morrow—happiest of happy days!
Would find *me* decked in chain and crimson baize—
But I'll dissemble—and, for chair of State,
Learn for a few short months to labour and to wait.

Then he recalled the topics of his speech,
Till, mutt'ring oft, he did New Bridge Street reach.
The Weaver's Tower then rising into view
Led him to feel sensations strangely new ;
For the demolished haunt of social Bats
Stood, lighted up from basement to its flats.
Such a reversal of old Nature's laws
Urged him, of course, to seek to learn the cause.

He stood awhile, uncertain what to do.
First, thought he would discretion's course pursue,
And homeward go. Then, that the better plan
Would be th' interior of the Tower to scan ;
And for that purpose walked across the street,
When further marvels did his vision greet.
Could waking dream his waking senses craze ?
The Public Library seemed all a-blaze !

'Tis strange, he said, at this weird hour of night,
That I should find *that* building very light!
I thought it heavy! But I'll try to see—
Ay—to the bottom of this mystery!
He reached the door, and raised his hand to knock,
But through his veins there ran a fearful shock—
Greater than that from battery galvanic—
Producing symptoms like those termed tetanic.

An unseen hand the door did open wide :
He found himself the vestibule inside.
Anon, he looked the Lending-Room within,
But no one came his usual smile to win.
The Books were ready for the Opening Day,
But no one deigned his rising fears to stay ;
Alarmed, he tried the faintest cry to utter,
But all his efforts ended in a stutter.

He wrung his hands like one in blank despair,
But drew the line at tearing out his hair ;
While beads of perspiration slowly oozed
From pores cuticular, and nerves refused
Their wonted work to do.   Transfixed he stood,
A prey to fears of dire Pandora's brood,
Till suddenly his eye did faintly trace
The outlines of a friendly form and face.

PLATE III.

XII.

What seemed a model of Canova's art,
Yet equally of Earth and Air a part—
Like haggard stone from some wild comet-land—
Appeared before him.   With an outstretched hand,
A wearied aspect and dull, jaded looks,
It pointed to the well-packed rows of books :
Men's brains, preserved, on patent shelving stored,
A cosmopolitan and goodly hoard.

XIII.

Behold, it said, the evidence of toil,
Of stern endurance born of Tyneside soil !
Some twenty thousand volumes now are here
With Catalogue exhaustive, full and clear.
My staff and I have done our work right well,
Though, sad to state—if I the truth may tell—
We all with Book-worm fever are worn out,
Or harassed with the Literary gout.

XIV.

A pause ensued.   The aerial Statue smiled—
The smile was bitter, with a dash of mild.
I have, it said, dead Authors of Romance
Invited to a Novel Light Seance !
Here, and to-night, Philosophers will come
With Scientists and Moralizers, glum,
Inventors, Poets, Travellers, and Scribes,
Of all the varied, best, and truest tribes.

You see my box-seat in the corner, there,
Pray, take an Order for its vacant chair.
The Actors, on this First Night of our Play,
Were of the best description in their day ;
So, be assured, no dangerous surprise
Will mar your pleasure—when the Spirits rise !
Which having with a subtle archness said,
The Chief-Librarian trotted home to bed.

Perplexed, the Doctor reached the well-known box :
An unseen hand its fast-closed door unlocks.
He then resolved to take a seat and wait,
Micawber like : a prisoner of State
He found himself. With feelings rather mixed,
He seemed as though hermetically fixed ;
For hand unseen had locked his prison's door,
And made the Chairman sadder than before.

He then essayed the half-glazed screen to scale,
Buoyed with the thought that only cravens fail—
And with that aim he tried to shift his chair,
But from his hands it floated into air !
Repeated efforts proved him quite unable
To climb the cabinet, which formed a table ;
For unseen hands—*vide* Romance of yore—
Laid the poor Doctor flat upon the floor.

He struggled with a will—with might and main—
An upright standing in the world to gain ;
But found, to his unspeakable surprise,
'Tis sometimes easier to fall than rise !
How long our hero *hors de combat* lay,
Has not been stated, but one fact we may
Record, having attained his normal elevation,
He saw that hands unseen had caused an alteration.

XIX.

Formed by an unknown, odd, and silent power,
A covered archway led to Carliol Tower,
Whence shades of long-departed Authors came
To view that latest temple of their fame !
In double file they glided in procession,
Before the screen which held him in possession,
And, as the Doctor peered into each face,
Pleasure's expression he could clearly trace.

XX.

A circumstance which claimed his keen attention,
We will, without apology, just mention.
'Twas this : Of all that most illustrious throng,
Not one seemed for a cause of strife to long ;
But all appeared discordant themes to smother,
And each to please and gratify another !
Strange ! that in life men other men decry,
And only cease contending when they die !

XXI.

Lord Bacon and Will Shakespeare led the way
To Chaucer, Barrow, Wycherley, and Gray.
These followed were by Bunyan and De Foe,
Who just preceded Howe and Allan Poe.
John Milton chatted freely with Tom Hood,
And Doctor Barth smiled pleasantly at Goode.
Ricardo, Arnold, Shelley, Baxter, Cheever,
Were paired with Moore, Ford, Sturm, Congreve, and Lever.

XXII.

Dean Swift, Buffon, and *Doctor Syntax*, Coombe,
With Dryden, Hook, and Watts, surveyed the room.
Macaulay, Gay, Burns, Rogers, and Voltaire,
Found friends in Young, Pope, Marlowe, Hume, and Blair ;
Sterne, Addison, Coleridge, and Stuart Mill,
In Webster, Smollett, Scrope, and Rowland Hill ;
While Suckling, Fielding, Rastell, and old Hooper,
Come trooping in with Browne, Horne, Scott, and Cooper.

XXIII.

Then Ravensworth's first Earl, so calm and grey,
Came in with Wilson and his *Pitman's Pay :*
While Cowper, Dalton, Jay, and Charles Knight
Fluttered with Goethe, Dick, Macneill, and White.
Will Cobbett came with Bishop Hall, his friend,
And Chesterfield with Bentham seemed to blend.
The third Napoleon looked quite charmed with Schiller,
And Lemon found a genial mate in Miller.

PLATE IV.

XXIV.

Sir Isaac Newton came with Doctor Franklin,
While Doctor Johnson fraternised with Macklin,
Bob Southey, Backhouse, Boswell, Byron, Gosse,
Filed in with Fuller, Brand, Hunt, Lamb, and Moss ;
Gibbon with Cranmer, Massinger with Whewell,
Dickens with Surtees, Bourne with Bishop Jewell,
Jerrold with Whately, Robertson with Taine,
Spenser with Tredgold, Chatterton with Blaine.

XXV.

Mackenzie, Warren, Faraday, and Knox,
Joined Butler, Hallam, Morrison, and Foxe,
Campbell and Grafton, Wilberforce and Gurney.
Horsley and Otway, Gregory and Burney,
Luther and Priestley, Ormerod and Paley,
Hazlitt and Irving, Potter and D'Israeli :
While Bishop Newton was obliged to hurry,
To overtake his dear friend Lindley Murray.

XXVI.

Gillray and Douce both seemed as full of mirth,
And fond of joking, as when on the earth
In mortal guise ; while Marryat and Tooke
Like schoolboys just released from school did look.
Old Overall with Milman jogged along,
And Greville coalesced with Count Grammont ;
The Percy Brothers had renewed their youth,
And various searchers had found out the truth.

Prevented by inexorable space,
We can't each Ghost's identity here trace,
Nor give a list of all that great array
Of Author-Spirits who had come to pay
An honour to the Town which had brought forth
Mark Akenside—sweet songster of the North !
Though different aims appeared their thoughts to sway,
They never tried to clog each other's way.

Some swarmed about the teeming rows of shelves,
Like airy, fairy, literary elves ;
While others—of a density much greater —
Sat perched upon the " Elliott Indicator."
But " North," who told the tale of *Margaret Lyndsay*,
The " Ettrick Shepherd," Lockhart, and De Quincey—
Four Spirits that once gave to *Maga* power !—
A night ambrosian held within the Tower.

While shades of Bats, departed, hovered round
Their famous guests, the *Blackwood* Ghosts were found
Descanting on the Spirit of the Time,
Which neither bends to Reason nor to Rhyme.
De Quincey termed all Politics a Mystery ;
John Wilson thought they helped to make up History ;
But Hogg and Lockhart took another course,
And, bridling discord, saddled neither horse.

XXX.

The great Professor was addressed by Hogg :
Some Politics are naethin' but a log
Aboot ane's neck—a tetherin'-post for Asses—
An' ne'er designed tae eelevate the masses !
Gi'e me a Library, an' ye may tak'
The Breetish Hoose o' Commons on yoor back—
Wi' a' its rantin,' roarin' deeclamashin—
I wud be first tae ceevilize the nashin.

XXXI.

In purer English, and in tones polite,
Then Lockhart answered : Friends and Bats, old Night
Is on her path to meet the youthful Day !
We'd better, till she next return, delay
The argument, and join our mutual friends
Within the Library. We owe amends
To them for lack of courtesy. Agreed !
And all passed from the Tower with aerial speed.

XXXII.

A close inspection of the volumes o'er,
Each Author-Shade descended to the floor ;
And Burton—old *Book-Hunter*, debonnair—
Cried : Silence, Spirits, order for the Chair,
Which now, I move, shall speedily be filled
By one in diplomatic bearing skilled.
The motion being seconded by Kames,
The Chair was forthwith taken by King James.

XXXIII.

The Chairman rose—a few feet in the air—
Coughed loudly thrice—hem'd—haw'd—and tugged his hair ;
A titter through the mute assembly ran,
Then Jamie plucked up courage, and began :
Friends, Countrymen, and Lovers—of a tome—
We've ne'er regretted that we left our home
In Holyrood [*hear, hear*] for London's town,
To—change a Scotch groat for an English crown.

XXXIV.

A Scot !—Of course we dearly loved to joke,
And into other people's business poke
Our nasal organ.   That, you will admit,
Was the correct thing !—not a little bit
Beneath the dignity of England's King !
And as our merchants to our shores did bring
A noxious weed—which reeked like chimneys vast—
We had to raise our kingly *Counterblast.*

XXXV.

Finding we did conspicuously inherit
Our mother's wisdom and our father's merit,—
Although a King !—we took to Authorship,
As readily as gulls in th' ocean dip.
It gives us therefore, sirs, the greatest pleasure,
To find Newcastle has got such a treasure
As our good " Works "—in ancient calf, complete—
To give the citizens a Royal treat.

PLATE V.

XXXVI.

Before we close our elegant oration,
We must express our highest approbation
Of all the efforts of the First Committee
To found a Library worthy of a City!
Our Royal thanks we also would convey
To those who have, in the remotest way,
Assisted while this Library was rearing.—
The Chairman then subsided amidst cheering.

XXXVII.

Another James—a Commoner—arose,
And to th' august assembly did disclose
An awful secret! Bending oft his head
Towards the Chairman, James—the second—said :
My "High and Mighty" namesake, in the Chair,
May't please your Majesty, a goodly share
Of pains I took to end what seemed a dead-lock,
And bring about to-morrow's happy wedlock.

XXXVIII.

Two hundred years ago, with zeal I kept
The Bodleian treasures ; and anon I've wept
If I but found a dog's-ear in a book.
At early morn—by day or night—by hook
Or crook—it ever was my great delight
To guard, with jealous care, from vulgar sight,
The pond'rous Folios which graced my racks,
With elephantine ridges on their backs.

In Spiritland—as modern writers shew—
We're not allowed, on principle, to throw
Aside the tastes that we acquired on earth,
Or habits fondly cherished from our birth.
More than we were, we must not hope to be!
And that, I find, is now the case with me.
A Bodleian Keeper of the good old school :
Librarians, modern, 'tis my pride to rule!

Of all the Libraries I go the round,
And where not wanted, there I may be found.
When badgering a luckless Chief-official,
I'm neither squeamish, slow, nor superficial.
Both Chairmen and Committees feel my sway,
Though some forget due deference to pay
To English Authors dead! Still, for the rest,
The adage, "Carpe diem," is the best.

When in the humour, or occasion suits,
I visit the Mechanics' Institutes
Throughout the country ; and, with grief I say,
The great majority do not display
A truly sound and vigorous vitality,
But rather dullness, or a cold formality!
If a disease we don't attempt to cure,
The patient must its penalties endure.

When David—once the Shepherd-youth intrepid—
Became, through maladies of age, decrepid,
The Court-physicians met in consultation,
And—with the usual courtly salutation—
Gave their opinion of the patient's case ;
Taking account of manners, times, and place.
That their prescription's sense may not miscarry,
I will translate it into English : Marry!

And so, we find, a damsel fair was caught,
Who to the aged sufferer was brought ;
A marriage-license being next procured,
King David's future comfort was secured!
Thus will it be, until Tom Campbell's last
And single man shall find his lines are cast
In places solitary ! Of man's mortal life,
The ills and troubles best are ended by a wife!

There is analogy the most complete
'Tween David's nuptials and that union, meet,
We meet to celebrate to-night. The old
Mechanics' Institute, worn-out and cold,
A heating-apparatus did require ;
To take the place of that Promethean fire
Which blazed awhile, then filled these rooms with smoke,
And ultimately left—a load of Coke!

XLV.

Two Doctors next appear upon the stage—
One looking sprightly, th' other's aspect sage—
The first, advised the Patient should be mated :
The second, Marriage-unions deprecated.
Gratuitous advisers, by the score,
The Patient's state then sadly did deplore.
While others, gifted with a second-sight,
Declared the weak old fellow sound and right !

XLVI.

Men differ must when Doctors disagree,
Or when advantages some fail to see
In what is called the Public Libraries' Act,
Which I would term a well-accomplished fact !
I will not further trespass on your time,
Save but to utter one more thought sublime :
No Scribbler may the Institute deride—
The Public Library is now his bride !

XLVII.

Then Goldsmith rose above the Spectral crowd.
I hope, he said, that I may be allowed—
With our most high and mighty Chair's approval,
And ere the dawn doth cause our quick removal
To other latitudes—a word or two.
Let us contrast the old times with the new.
To follow Letters, now, is quite delectable,
But Authors, then, were scarcely thought respectable.

XLVIII.

The Publisher despised the Man of Letters,
And held him fast in worse than iron fetters.
Now—just to give to converse a variety—
The Author takes his place in good society.
For this great change our thanks are largely due
To Libraries private, public, old and new!—
But, leaving Goldsmith eloquent and wise,
We will return to one who heedless lies.

XLIX.

The Doctor, having conquered false alarm,
Soon realised that not the slightest harm
Was meant towards him, other than mild durance—
His very prison gave to him assurance!—
And, as each Speaker did at periods pause,
He rapped, instead of shouting, his applause.
But when at length the rhetoric grew stronger,
He felt he really could not stand it longer.

L.

Like mouse confined too long in household trap.
He tried to stifle sorrow with a nap;
So, sitting on the chair, he raised his feet
Upon the table and did thus entreat
Old Somnus' aid, who came to his relief.
What followed afterwards exceeds belief!
Scarce had the Doctor what he sought for found,
Than through the room notes direful did resound!

LI.

A stranger's present, angry Spirits cried,
While others to the Sleeper quickly hied,
Intent to know whence could such sounds proceed.
They seized upon him, formed a Court with speed,
And then arraigned him, shaking in each limb,
While the indictment was rehearsed to him.
The counts were, first, a total want of gumption ;
And, secondly, a piece of gross presumption.

LII.

Rash being, said the almost furious King,
How is it that you have thus dared to bring
Your mortal presence here, unbidden too—
Of stupid acts the stupidest to do—
And, not content with daring to intrude
Upon our Council, you must be so rude
As with contempt to treat our Chair : yea more,
For you not only go to sleep, but snore !

LIII.

Like one awaking from a death-like trance,
The Doctor with suspicious eye did glance
Among the Spirits ; but not one appeared
Inclined to shield him from the fate he feared.
Meeting but scowls on every side, he tries,
With downcast visage, to apologise :
Although I'm guilty—and I dearly rue it—
" Honest and Truthful " egg'd me on to do it.

The King replies: Who dares to lay a claim
To such a pseudonym, to such a name?
We've always thought that mankind's various schools
Form but two classes—those of knaves and fools.
But we must see this prodigy, forsooth:
This costly specimen of native Truth!
Will any Spectre kindly volunteer
To bring the precious sample safely here?

I will, your Majesty. The name of Smith
To Truth and Honesty is kin and kith;
And Adam Smith was the proud name I bore
Ere I had landed on the Stygian shore.
While greater Works are, like their Authors, dead,
My *Wealth of Nations* still is sold and read:
Proving conclusively· though some may mock it—
A subject of much interest is the pocket.

That mortal, whom you now desire to see,
Is an Economist well known to me,
One of the family in fact; and so,
To fetch him, I'll to lofty Elswick go.
The speaker bowed, then vanished with a will,
Mounted o'er housetops, soared up Westgate Hill,
Entered the room where the Financier lay
In troubled sleep, and carried him away!

High in the air the Phantom bore his freight,
Nor overladen was with such a weight ;
As trusty nurse conveys the child with care,
So did the messenger his burden bear.
And forced the man of figures forth to roam :
A spirited proceeding, *a la Home !*
Thus did they speed above the silent Town,
Without the slightest fear of tumbling down.

LVIII.

As quick as thought the Court was reached and entered,
While eyes therein were on the ceiling centred :
For through the roof an opening had been made
Down which the Spectre came and deftly laid
His charge unconscious prone. A kick, a shake,
Caused it to stand erect and wide-a-wake.
The great one gazed around with wondering look
As judge and jury brought his acts to book.

LIX.

The Prisoners being severally charged,
King James upon presumptious crime enlarged :
You must have known, the angry Monarch said,
That Folly skips where Wisdom fears to tread ;
And proud Ambition seldom can be found
On honest Virtue's safe and solid ground :
But Fortune's slippery glacier doth explore,
Until it falls and sinks to rise no more.

LX.

One Culprit bold, defiant, almost rude.
The other self-convicted, downcast stood.
You both plead guilty, sternly said the King,
If either of you have now anything
To say why sentence should be longer stayed,
Let your excuse be urgent, not delayed,
And also brief, for Brevity is wise :
Ere dawns the light of day on our assize.

LXI.

Hoping he might the ghostly circle "square,"
"Honest and truthful," with a lofty air,
Went into calculations, by the score,
To demonstrate that two times two are four ;
Which having noted, in a tone of grim
Impatience, thus the Court came down on him :
Though you for figures are a perfect glutton,
Truth does not always need the aid of Hutton !

LXII.

The Doctor having waited till his friend
Had in his speech made one good point, the end,
Braced himself up for the unequal strife
Against hard fate, like one who swims for life.
With eyes depressed and nervous twitching hands
He wanly, shyly, humbly, sadly stands :
His *tout ensemble*, gesture and expression,
Making a very forcible impression.

My Lord, I wish to say a word or two,
Before the sentence is pronounced by you.
'Tis true that Zeal Discretion's pace out ran,
For Zeal was jockeyed by this other man.
I, on Discretion, was not in the race :
We did not even so much as get a place.
Besides, my Lord, think of that famous line,
" To err is human, to forgive divine !"

Whoever of a phantom is in quest
Will find his life a period of unrest.
Fame was the phantom that I daily sought,
And hitherto the search has nothing brought
To me but opposition, snubs, and care—
Who will next occupy the Mayor's Chair
If I am lodged in durance ?   Surely, then,
Newcastle must have *Cauld Cail het again !*

Fain would I plead—for poor Newcastle's sake—
That you would now upon me pity take ;
Long years I've laboured, exercised much tact,
For the adoption of the *Libraries' Act !*
The goal is reached, ere sets to-morrow's sun,
The prize—a Public Library—will be won !
But if they find that I am kept away,
What will Bret Harte, Mayne Reid, and Mason say ?

LXVI.

Then slowly rose the Monarch from his chair,
The Court's dread sentence sternly to declare :
We're much surprised to find one Prisoner make
A claim for mercy for Newcastle's sake.
Prating of Law, has her wise Corporation
Extended Equity to Learning's station ;
Severed its leading-strings of reddest tape :
Or mercy shown towards poor Doctor Snape ?

LXVII.

We sentence you to act as Toll-Collectors
From pompous Preachers, Pipers, and Projectors,
Entering Newcastle, on her sons to trade,
Till ten times o'er the Doctor's pension's paid !
Both Prisoners quaked with inward, abject fear,
When they the dreadful doom pronounced did hear ;
But one resolved his fate to firmly meet,
And—*found himself a Freeman in the street !*

LXVIII.

He trembled in each limb, he sighed, he shivered ;
His very card-case in his pocket quivered !
The spectral light had faded with the Tower ;
His watch refused to register the hour.
I was a Doctor once, he coldly said,
A surgeon born and a physician bred ;
Of Novocastria a native, resident !
He turned, and met the Ex-Mechanics' President.

Why! What has kept you out of bed last night?
The comer asked in cheery tones. A sight!
Enough to cause one's hair to stand on end,
Or Hellespont with Whittle Dene to blend!
The Chairman said, and then in full related
All that we have now in our story stated.
I see, his friend replied, you need repose :
Of Spirits you have had an over-dose.

A fringe of faintest light on cloudlets grey
Did herald the approach of dawning day :
That day designed to mark an era new
To Novocastria's sons and daughters true!
When Knowledge—free, attainable—may seem
More than a rich man's pride or poor man's dream!
So, smiling to his Æsculapian brother,
Each Doctor said, GOOD MORNING to the other.

PLATE VIII.

www.ingramcontent.com/pod-product-compliance
Lightning Source LLC
Chambersburg PA
CBHW022204020726
47496CB00008B/2879